Lindsa
Christm
Love, Gr
D1448027

THE FOREVER WREATH

Story by Camille J. Bolinger

Hand-carved Illustrations by Paul F. Bolinger

ISBN 0-9632777-6-6   Library of Congress Catalog Card Number 92-081305

Printed in Japan   First edition, October 1992

                        1 2 3 4 5 6 7 8 9 10 / 97 96 95 94 93 92

We dedicate this book to our son, Jake Bear Bolinger, who has lived this story amid the carvings and confusion. He has inspired us with his joyfulness and has kept the child within us alive.

THIS BOOK BELONGS TO:

4

Tucked in a mountain valley, far from a busy city and deep in the woods, there sat a small, quaint cottage.

This little house was a happy place indeed. It was the color of a soft blue sky. The cheery front windows faced a grove of old fir trees. An inviting red-brick path wound past snow-covered juniper bushes to a small front porch. Through the gaily decorated door, lived a jolly woodcarver, his wife, and their young son.

It was exactly the kind of place where something special could happen at Christmas.

Each and every morning the woodcarver climbed up on a sturdy stool before his old workbench. After carefully sharpening his knives and chisels, he carved exquisite Father Christmas figures for people living in the far-off city.

The woodcarver's son watched his father as he slowly and carefully chipped and cut away at the strong, straight wood. Often the small boy dreamed of becoming a woodcarver himself.

At the end of the day the boy helped his father sweep up the wood chips that lay scattered beneath the bench. The boy was always happy to work with his father.

The carvings were not complete without their coat of paint. It was the woodcarver's wife who used her skill as an artist to color the hand-carved figures.

She often worked at the kitchen table, skillfully blending oil paints on her palette. When she had just the right colors, back and forth her long-handled brush would go as she painted the unique Father Christmas carvings.

The special character of each piece began to show itself as she worked. Finally, with a touch of brilliant blue, the eyes twinkled to life.

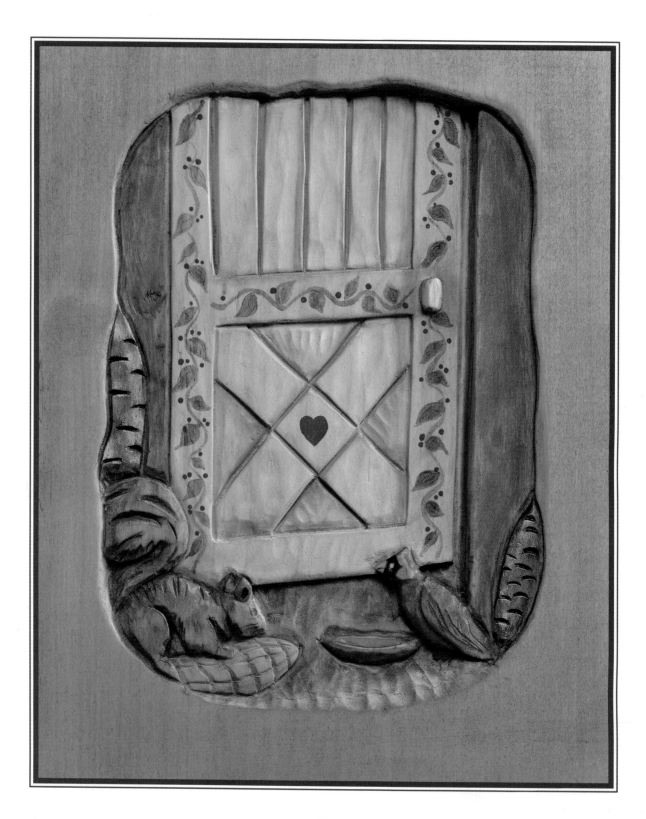

Throughout the year the family spent many hours working together, completing the Father Christmas figures.

They also took time to enjoy the peaceful surroundings of their little cottage. The beautiful woods and many forest friends gave them great pleasure.

Every morning they opened the cottage door to scatter seeds for the birds and squirrels. Often the deer could be seen using the salt lick the family had built at the edge of the woods.

After finishing their evening meal, the family set out left-over vegetable greens for the rabbits and crusts of bread for the raccoons' nightly visit.

Now, the woodcarver and his family were not the only ones lucky enough to live in the cozy little cottage.

A small, furry mouse listened each day to the tap…tap…tap of the woodcarver's mallet. He had gnawed a hole in the kitchen wall and had made a warm, snug home inside. His nest contained pieces of old fabric, some wood shavings and a collection of string. Here the mouse lived very comfortably.

The woodcarver and his family knew that the little mouse lived with them, and loved them. Each morning they set out cheese in a small dish beside the opening in the wall.

The little cottage mouse often overheard the woodcarver and his family talk about how important it was for them to create the Father Christmas figures.

The figure might be that of an old man, hooded against the cold with a walking stick in one hand. Perhaps it would resemble a tall bishop dressed in grand, red robes. Whatever the design, the Father Christmas carvings recalled the centuries-old story of Saint Nicholas, who is remembered for his kindness and generosity toward everyone he met.

The woodcarver and his wife believed that their carvings could touch hearts everywhere, rekindling this spirit of love.

One particular afternoon, from behind a mallet on the workbench, the mouse overheard the woodcarver tell his family that many people wanted carvings this year. The family would have to work steadily until Christmas day. Sadly, they would have no time left to decorate their cottage in honor of the holiday season.

The wife of the woodcarver knew that their work must be finished. Nonetheless, she felt that Christmas would not be as wondrous without decorations for the cottage. She was especially sorry for their young son after seeing him blink back his tears. She knew how terribly disappointed he felt.

O h," thought the little mouse to himself, "A Christmas without decorations…how sad that would be!"

The cottage mouse knew there must be a way he could help these people who had always been so good to him and the other animals. He started thinking and by the next morning he had a plan he was sure would work.

At dawn the mouse squeezed through a thin crack in the cottage wall to the snow-covered ground outside. He immediately sought out his closest friends to tell them of his plan, and to get their help.

By midday the mouse was standing on an up-ended wooden bucket. He was sheltered from the lightly falling snow by the green boughs of an old fir tree. Gathered around him were White Rabbit, Cardinal Red, Brown Squirrel, Deer Amber, and the Raccoon family.

As his forest friends listened quietly, the mouse told how the family had no time to decorate their cottage in honor of the Christmas season. The animals were especially touched when he described the little boy's tears.

The mouse reminded his friends how much they themselves had enjoyed the cottage Christmas decorations in the past.

Deer Amber declared that he would miss peeking through the cottage window to gaze upon the beautifully decorated tree.

Cardinal Red thought fondly of the soft glow that the star atop the tree cast through the forest. Others now chimed in recalling the fresh green garland draped around the cottage door and the tiny wooden angels that had hung in the many-paned windows.

Of course, none of them could forget the yearly goodwill wreath that the family covered with apples, nuts, and suet for the animals' special enjoyment.

While they were all still taken with these memories, the mouse cleared his throat and began to speak slowly and carefully.

The woodcarver and his family have been kind to each of us. It is time for us to do something special for them," the mouse declared. "If we use our unique abilities and work together, we can make a lovely gift."

The gift the mouse proposed would hang on the cottage door... the animals could make a Christmas wreath for the family.

Brown Squirrel was the first to volunteer. He had spent the brisk fall days collecting and storing nuts for the winter. Now he would search all his favorite hiding places and select the best hickory nuts, chestnuts, and black walnuts he could find.

White Rabbit had listened carefully to all that had been said, her long, soft ears bent slightly forward. Suddenly her eyes brightened. She fluffed her round tail and hopped quickly to her home beneath the old fir tree.

No one could guess what White Rabbit would bring for the wreath. When she returned, she held in her front paws a lovely pastel bouquet. Through the summer she had gathered fresh flowers. Bunches of colorful statice in pink, yellow, and purple had hung, upside down, in her warren to dry. Now White Rabbit's dried flowers would bring color to the wreath.

Deer Amber, the strongest of the mouse's friends, used his sharp hooves to dig beneath the crusted snow for runners of fresh ground pine. The greenery he found would form the body of the wreath when twisted around a circle fashioned from grape vines.

Cardinal Red scoured the woods, flying to the tops of the highest trees on his sturdy wings. He searched for clusters of bright red berries and shiny sprigs of holly. With these treasures in his beak, he flew back to the mouse. Again and again he flew until just enough holly and berries had been collected to decorate the wreath.

The cottage mouse scurried back to his nest to gather plenty of string to be used to bind the wreath together. The Raccoon family with their nimble fingers would assemble the Christmas wreath that night.

Under the glow of a full moon, the raccoons worked steadily. First they wrapped and tied the ground pine around a circle of grape vines. Then they added holly twigs and berries along with a variety of nuts. Finally the colorful dried flowers were tucked into the wreath.

As the first morning light filled the woods, the glorious wreath was completed. The animals stood back to admire it. They all agreed…it was perfect! They were proud that together they had produced such a beautiful gift.

The animals carried the wreath across the snow and carefully placed it on the cottage porch. Quickly they each hid nearby to watch the discovery of their gift.

The woodcarver's son opened the cottage door to toss a handful of wild seeds to the ground. Suddenly he stopped, his arm in mid-air, as he spied the wreath leaning against the side of the house.

Excited, he called to his mother and father. When they reached the door, they too saw the lovely wreath.

Surprised and puzzled at how this beautiful wreath came to be, the woodcarver quietly looked about. His wife asked who could possibly know how much such a wreath would mean to them this year.

I know!" the little boy shouted with glee. "Look, there, in the snow! See the tracks leading up to our door?"

Sure enough, there on the new fallen snow the family could make out the many tracks left by their forest friends.

The large, jolly woodcarver bent down on one knee and carefully lifted the wreath. He turned and hung it from the nail in the center of the bare cottage door. The animals, watching from behind the trees, saw large, ploppy tears roll down the face of this big man as he put up the handsome wreath.

The family was deeply touched by the thoughtfulness of the animals. They promised one another that they would thank these kind friends in a very special way.

The gift wreath still hung on the door the following spring. One morning, the woodcarver and his family stepped out onto their front porch. The young boy, who had grown taller over the winter months, reached up and lifted the now-weathered wreath from the nail on the cottage door.

In its place the woodcarver hung another. The new wreath was carved from wood and painted with bright colors. The family had hand-crafted it to look exactly like the one the animals had made for them. There was one important difference though…in the middle of this wreath was a carefully carved likeness of the little mouse.

This gift of love would hang forever on the cottage door to say thank you to the mouse and his forest friends.

SPECIAL ACKNOWLEDGMENTS

The road from carving as a hobby to carving as a life has taken years. Along the way, many people have influenced, supported, and helped us. We thank these special people:

Our parents, Himes and Betty Bolinger, and Cy and Lola Jacobs, for their gift of love; Rod and MaryBeth Giske for the idea of writing and carving a book.

Jean LemMon, editor-in-chief of *Country Home* magazine, for discovering our work and for her many letters of encouragement.

Our longtime friends, Peter and Laura Dunn,
Ron and Coreen Lee, and Joe and Joan Shane,
who have tolerated the chips, paint and endless
hours of discussion; and our neighbors and friends
at Enchanted Valley who have been like family.

Kathy Revello of Gump's, and Nancy Hannum
of Neiman-Marcus, who appreciated our work
and helped us become successful.

The putting together of this book, like the story
itself, was a collective effort. We thank these
people who helped us turn our ideas into a book:
Jayne King; Joe Shane; Todd Tsukushi of Santa
Cruz Photographics; Felicia Rice of Moving Parts
Press; and Nancy Enge of Ajax Design Group.

ABOUT THE BOOK

The inspiration for *The Forever Wreath* came from the life of woodcarving and painting the Bolingers have made for themselves.

The idea for this book came during a Christmas visit to snowy eastern Washington state. The first draft was discussed and written down during the Bolinger's fourteen-hour drive south to their home in California.

The story was refined, drawings made, and finally the illustrations were hand-carved at Three Bear's Cottage, the family cabin in the redwood-covered hills of Santa Cruz.

The Forever Wreath is a timeless story of the same heirloom quality as the Father Christmas carvings. It is a book to be treasured and passed from one generation to the next.